**W**hen 10-year-... stumbles upon a mysterious alien device in the woods one summer, little does he realise that his life is set to change - forever.

As soon as the watch-like Omnitrix quite literally gets a grip on him, Ben discovers it gives him the ability to transform into 10 different alien super-beings, each one with awesome powers!

Using the Omnitrix to cause superpowered mischief turns out to be fun, but will Ben learn to use his might to fight for good?

**READ ON AND FIND OUT . . .**

# MEET THE CHARACTERS

## BEN TENNYSON
THE EVERYDAY KID WHO CAN'T HELP GOING HERO!

## GWEN TENNYSON
BEN'S VERBAL SPARRING PARTNER AND COUSIN

## GRANDPA MAX
THERE'S MORE TO HIM THAN MEETS THE EYE . . .

## VILGAX
THIS POWER-HUNGRY MANIAC GOT OUT OF BED THE WRONG SIDE!

## KEVIN 11
SUPER DRAIN

## GREYMATTER
SUPER BRAIN!

## RIPJAWS
NEVER BITES OFF MORE THAN HE CAN CHEW

## WILDMUTT
BEWARE OF THE DOG . . .

## XLR8
HE'S A GR8 M8 AND HE'S NEVER L8

## FOUR ARMS
ALWAYS PACKS A PUNCH OR FOUR!

## HEATBLAST
TOO HOT TO HANDLE!

## DIAMONDHEAD
THIS GUY DEFINITELY CUTS IT

## STINKFLY
THIS INSECT LIKES TO KEEP BUZZY

## UPGRADE
HE'S REALLY INTO COMPUTERS!

First published by Parragon in 2010

Parragon
Queen Street House
4 Queen Street
Bath BA1 1HE, UK

ISBN: 978-1-4454-0965-8

Printed in Australia

BEN 10™

TRUTH

+

FRAMED

Parragon

Bath · New York · Singapore · Hong Kong · Cologne · Delhi · Melbourne

# CHAPTER ONE

# MANY YEARS AGO . . .

**H**igh in the mountains, in the heart of a huge forest, a hidden missile-launching platform slowly began to slide open. Inside, a nuclear warhead – one of the most devastating weapons on the planet – lay motionless.

Suddenly, a blinding beam of yellow light stretched down from above, bathing the missile in its strange, twinkling glow. With a creaking and groaning of metal, the weapon tore free of the platform and began to soar upwards into the dark night sky.

❋ ❋ ❋

# AWOOGA! AWOOGA!

A screeching alarm echoed through the corridors of the missile base. Red light bulbs flashed into life on the grey metal walls, casting a spooky glow over the entire underground complex.

'Security breach!' warned an urgent computer voice. 'Red alert!'

The base commander skidded round the door frame and ran into the command room. A soldier sat at the control desk, anxiously pressing at flashing buttons. On the display screen in front of him, six more missiles shot up from the ground.

'I didn't authorise a launch!' boomed the commander. 'Abort! Abort!'

'We're not launching the nukes, sir!' replied the soldier, frantically flicking switches. 'Something's pulling them out of their holders!'

✵ ✵ ✵

With a **WHOOSH**, yet another nuclear missile was dragged from its mooring by the yellow beam. Up, up it went, before being swallowed by a hatch in the bottom of a large, heavily armoured alien battleship.

Three more warheads soared upwards, and three more after that. Each one was quickly pulled into the bowels of the alien ship.

❈ ❈ ❈

An explosion ripped through the inside of the missile base, tearing a thick metal door from its hinges and filling the area with choking black smoke.

A platoon of armed soldiers stood ready, their weapons trained on the wide hole in the wall. Their fingers twitched on their guns' triggers. It was difficult to see through the smoke, but it looked as if something had moved.

The air hissed as a blast of red-hot energy erupted from within the cloud. It hit the closest soldier square in the chest, throwing him off his feet. He hit the ground, unconscious.

The other soldiers braced themselves, ready for combat. Before they had a chance to open fire, another round of laser blasts burst through the smoke. In less than a second, they and their guns had clattered noisily on to the metal floor.

Two robotic drones hovered through the black haze, their weapons scanning for any more targets. Following behind them was a hulking brute of an alien. His beard of thick, slimy tentacles twitched as he stalked along the corridor.

He was Vilgax, the most feared creature in the entire known universe.

Vilgax strode across to the nearest nuclear missile and studied it. His mouth curled into a grin, revealing two rows of razor-sharp teeth.

'Primitive,' he growled. 'But destructive enough.'

## ZZZZZZZAP!

As the alien finished speaking, a bright-blue laser beam fizzled through the air beside his head, and one of his robotic drones exploded in a spectacular fireball. Vilgax spun round, fists clenched, only for a second bolt of energy to strike him. Its force pushed him backwards, away from the missiles, but otherwise the alien was unhurt.

'You!' he hissed, his eyes narrowed.

A figure stepped from the shadows, his face hidden by the helmet of his protective suit. He clutched a large rifle, strange lights blinking along its side.

Behind him, a smaller man stepped forwards. Though he was dressed the same, the second man was armed with a sleek handgun. His movements were less confident than those of the first man; he seemed edgy and nervous.

'It's over, Vilgax,' said the first man, his voice strong and commanding.

'You're going down!' chirped his younger-sounding colleague.

Vilgax slowly began to advance on the two men, his fists still tightly clenched.

'Many have tried,' he snarled. 'None have succeeded.'

'Until now, slimeball!' yelled the man with the pistol. He leaped forward, firing wild laser blasts at the alien.

'Phil! Wait!' the first man cried, but it was too late. Vilgax threw himself over the rain of energy beams, and flipped over in mid-air. Phil looked up just in time for the alien's foot to connect with his head. With a thud, his helmet hit the ground.

The first man watched helplessly as Vilgax twisted Phil round and used him as a human shield. In one swift movement, the alien tore the laser pistol from his prisoner's hand. Phil gulped nervously as it was pressed against his head.

Nearby, the second robot drone scuttled over to one of the few remaining nuclear missiles. It inserted a probe spike into the launch controls and began transmitting data. The screen on the controls blinked into life, and the words 'Launch ready' lit up the console.

'Back away,' Vilgax hissed, 'or watch one of your main cities be destroyed!'

The man with the rifle hesitated, his gun still pointed at the monstrous alien. Vilgax pressed his stolen gun harder against the side of Phil's head.

'Put the weapon down,' he barked. 'NOW!'

The man let his rifle clatter to the floor. Vilgax watched as the man kicked it to one side.

'You can't just let him get away!' yelped Phil, struggling against Vilgax's grip.

Beneath his helmet, the man smirked. 'Never said I would, kid.' He threw up his arm a bolt of energy screeched from it, hitting Vilgax before the alien could react.

Stunned, Vilgax released his grip on the gun. Phil aimed a crunching elbow blow backwards into the alien's ribs, and quickly ducked free of his grip.

'You're too late!' Vilgax hissed. Behind him, the nuclear missile roared into life and began to shudder and shake.

'Wrong! My timing's perfect,' corrected the man in the helmet. Stepping forwards, he flicked his rifle up into his hands and fired. A blob of thick, black goo shot from the barrel.

As the stuff hit Vilgax, it expanded and wrapped round him. The force of the collision knocked him backwards into his robot drone, and the two found themselves glued to the missile by the oily goo.

'NOOOOOO!' Vilgax roared, struggling helplessly as the missile screamed skyward.

'What are you doing?' demanded Phil, as the other man ran across to the control panel and began pressing buttons.

'Sending Vilgax out with a bang!' came the reply.

They looked up through the launch hatch and watched the missile head off course. Just before it collided with Vilgax's ship, the alien let out a loud, bellowing cry: 'TENNYSON!'

High in the mountains, above a huge, sprawling forest, an alien battleship exploded with an ear-shattering **BAD-OOOOM!**

## CHAPTER TWO

# HAVOCBEAST BY NAME . . .

In the passenger seat of The Rust Bucket, Ben Tennyson's eyes were wide with wonder. His cousin, Gwen, sat at the campervan's cramped dining table. Both of them were staring at their Grandpa Max in the driving seat. He had just finished telling them how he and his partner, Phil, had once battled Vilgax, and they could hardly believe their ears.

'And then – **KABLAMMO!**' Grandpa Max continued. 'No more Vilgax.' He glanced across at his grandson. 'Or so I thought.'

'Whoa!' gasped Ben. 'You were a hero!'

Grandpa Max shook his head. 'I was just a guy doing a job.'

'Excuse me,' asked Gwen, 'but exactly what was that job?'

Her grandfather sighed. He'd never told anyone about his old career before, but he was determined to be honest with his grandchildren.

'We called ourselves "The Plumbers",' he began. 'Officially, we didn't exist. We were the guys who fixed the problems no one else could. Extraterrestrial, extrasensory, extraordinary . . .'

'So all this time I've been going hero, I've really been following in your footsteps,' said Ben. He thought about this for a few moments, then grinned. 'I'm a Plumber in training!'

'And you knew about the watch the whole time?' demanded Gwen.

'Not really,' Grandpa Max assured her. 'Just rumour and scuttlebutt.' He glanced down at the Omnitrix on his grandson's arm. 'I was as surprised as you guys when it turned up.'

'You always told us we could tell you anything, Grandpa Max,' said Gwen. She leaned her head on one hand and stared out of the window. The sun was just beginning to set over the carved stone heads of the world-famous Mount Rushmore. 'Guess you didn't feel the same.'

Before Grandpa Max could reply, a wailing of sirens split the evening air. Wrenching the wheel, he pulled The Rust Bucket over on to the side of the road as a procession of police cars, fire engines and ambulances thundered by.

'All right!' cried Ben. 'Could be a chance for the Plumbers to go back to work!'

Gwen snorted. 'You should start by unclogging that hairball from your brain, Mr Plumber.'

'You're just jealous cos you're not part of the family business,' Ben replied, turning to stick his tongue out at his cousin.

'There is no "family business",' said
Grandpa Max dismissively. 'My hero days were
over a long time ago.'

'Well, mine are just getting started!' Ben
crowed, throwing open the door of The Rust
Bucket.

'Ben, wait!' Grandpa Max called, but
Ben was already outside, twisting the dial
on the Omnitrix. Whenever he needed to get
somewhere fast, there was one alien he could
always rely on.

'Time to XLR8!'

As Ben slammed his hand down on the

watch, a familiar cloud of green energy wrapped itself round him. Immediately, he began to change. His legs stretched. His arms grew. His feet formed into flippers.

Wait. Flippers?!

'Awww, Ripjaws?' he groaned. 'What a rip off!'

There was no way he could run after the police cars now. Still, he'd learned long ago that being a hero sometimes meant making the most of a bad situation.

As a fire engine screamed by, Ripjaws reached out a webbed hand and caught hold of a ladder. Clinging on tightly, he let the speeding vehicle carry him towards the unknown emergency that lay ahead.

�֍ ✖ ✖

Brakes screeching, the emergency vehicles pulled up outside a large hotel. Dozens of well-dressed guests huddled in groups outside, nervously glancing across at the building.

'There's some kind of creature inside!' yelped the hotel manager, as the last of the fire engines arrived on the scene. 'It's tearing up the place!'

He stopped, mid-panic, as a sudden torrent of water began to fall like heavy rain from above. Looking up, the manager gasped with shock. Standing on top of the closest fire engine, Ripjaws was soaking up the spray from the hose he was holding.

'Sorry,' said the alien. 'Just needed to moisturise.'

Without another word, Ripjaws somersaulted down from the roof of the vehicle and landed with a faint **SCHLOP** on the soaking-wet ground. Watched by dozens of startled onlookers, he sprinted over to the hotel's double doors and pushed them open.

Splintered furniture lay everywhere. Articles of luggage were scattered across the floor, most of them torn wide open. Clothes spilled from within the damaged cases, and those too were ripped to shreds. Of everything in the lobby, only two stone pillars and an impressive marble fountain remained intact.

'OK,' demanded Ripjaws, stepping in and letting the doors swing closed behind him. 'Who's the punk giving us "creatures" a bad name?'

A low, rumbling groan echoed around the lobby. A savage-looking alien known as a Havocbeast stepped from the shadows, snapping at the air with its pincer-like claws. Its eyes burned a dark, ominous red, and from its mouth hung long, thick strands of extraterrestrial drool.

Ripjaws blinked and peered down at the Havocbeast. The Havocbeast, in turn, looked up at him. And up. And up, until it almost fell over backwards.

The tiny alien snarled as Ripjaws roared with laughter. He could hardly believe that so much destruction could be caused by something barely bigger than a basketball!

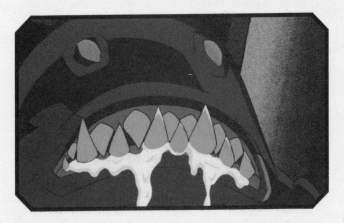

The Havocbeast snatched a lump of rubble from the ruined lobby floor and launched it at Ripjaws, smacking him hard in the head.

Ripjaws glared at the little creature. 'You picked the wrong day to be an alien, pal!'

He launched himself at the Havocbeast, arms outstretched, ready to scoop up the tiny critter. Too late!

**THUD!** Ripjaws landed hard on the spot where the creature had stood. From high up on the nearest stone pillar, it was the Havocbeast's turn to laugh. Its strange, high-pitched snigger only made Ripjaws angrier.

The Havocbeast threw itself from the pillar. Curling up into a ball, it landed in the ornamental fountain with a **SPLOSH**. It quickly popped back up, its cheeks bulging.

**SQUIRT!** The miniature alien giggled happily as it spat a mouthful of water in Ripjaws' face. Ben's alien form absorbed the liquid into his scaly skin, drawing strength from it as he watched the Havocbeast scurry away.

'That's just a breath of fresh air to me,' he said, before setting off in pursuit of the tiny terror.

※ ※ ※

Outside the hotel, a campervan coughed and spluttered into the car park. Before the engine had shuddered to a stop, The Rust Bucket's doors flew open, and Grandpa Max and Gwen dashed out.

When she spotted the manager, Gwen stopped, scratched her head and asked, 'Did anyone happen to see a giant talking fish come by here?'

※ ※ ※

Back inside the building, Ripjaws crept along the corridors, searching for any trace of the Havocbeast.

Edging backwards, he scanned the shadows for movement. Halfway down a corridor, he bumped into something large.

Spinning on the spot, he came face to face with a middle-aged man holding a very big gun.

'Aaargh! Who are you?' they both cried at once. 'Who am I?' they each demanded. 'Who are you?'

With a shrug, the man suddenly raised his weapon and fired. The blast sent Ripjaws sprawling along the floor. He thudded to a stop against a wall.

The armed man stepped forwards, his rifle raised. Strange lights blinked along its side as he took aim at Ripjaws.

'Looks like today's my lucky day,' he sneered. 'Two aliens for the price of one!'

# CHAPTER THREE

# AN OLD FRIEND

**R**ipjaws groaned as he tried to sit up. The blast had taken a lot out of him. If he could only rest for a few moments, he'd be fine.

But the man with the gun wasn't about to give him time to recover. He stepped closer to Ripjaws, the rifle aimed at the hero's head.

A sudden inhuman roar made the man whip round. The Havocbeast was approaching, its tiny arms stretched out, ready to attack. The gunman's protective body armour creaked as he craned his neck to look down at Ripjaws.

'Just sit tight, fishstick,' he spat. 'I'll be back in a minute.'

The Havocbeast screamed and ran for

its life as a burst of laser fire scorched the floor around it. Grinning, the gunman set off firing wildly.

Slowly, his arms shaking from the effort, Ripjaws reached up and pulled a jug of iced water down from the desk above his head. The cool, clear liquid poured down on him, instantly giving him a recharge.

'Ahhh,' he sighed. 'You've got to love room service!'

Not far off, the armed man crept cautiously along the corridor, searching for any sign of the Havocbeast. The alien was small and fast, but it couldn't hide forever.

Suddenly, a high bookcase began to wobble back and forth. Too late to run, the man threw up his arms for protection as hundreds of books rained down on top of him, followed by the heavy wooden book case itself – *THUMP!*

The Havocbeast leaped down from the fallen shelves and danced with delight.

As it celebrated, a large metal safe clanked down over it, trapping it. It banged angrily against the walls of its prison, but they were too strong to break.

'Not bad for a fishstick, huh?' said Ripjaws, watching the man struggle beneath the bookcase.

Before he could decide whether to help him or not, the Omnitrix began to flash red. **BLEEP BLEEP BLEEP BLEEEEP!** In the blink of an eye, Ripjaws transformed back to plain old Ben. Luckily, the gunman hadn't seen the change, and Ben was able to leave the scene before the man could pull himself free.

He was running so fast he almost smacked straight into Grandpa Max, who was standing with Gwen just inside the hotel doorway.

'Ben, are you all right?'

'Barely!' cried Ben. 'Some nutjob in there nearly roasted me!' He glanced back along the corridor just as the armed man dragged himself free of the shelves. The man's eyes almost popped out of his head when he spotted Grandpa Max.

'Max!' he gasped.

A broad grin spread across Grandpa Max's face. 'Phil!' he said, beaming.

Ben watched on, shocked, as the two old friends hugged warmly.

'You know this guy, Grandpa Max?'

'You could say that,' said Phil, nodding. 'We used to be partners.'

Ben glanced across at Gwen. This day was just full of surprises.

※ ※ ※

With a grunt of effort, Phil heaved the heavy
safe into the back of his worn-out old car, the
Havocbeast thudding against the inside.

The metal box safely tucked in the
boot, Phil gave the car a loving pat. 'Yeah,' he
admitted, catching Grandpa Max's stare, 'she's
not much to look at, but she's better than that
old rust bucket of a campervan you used to
drive.'

Grandpa Max smiled and quickly changed
the subject. 'So, how are you?'

'Pretty good considering I just bagged a
Havocbeast. Seems like old times.'

'You bagged it?' Ben snapped. 'As if! It
was Rip–'

Grandpa Max stepped in front of
Ben before he could give too much away.
'Havocbeast, huh?' he said quickly. 'Haven't
seen one of those since the one we caught
terrorising Denver years ago.'

'Yeah, well, good thing I was around,' said Phil, smiling. 'You know, once a Plumber, always a Plumber.' His eyes lit up as he had an idea. 'Ever think about getting back in the game, Max? You know, relive the glory days?'

'No, thanks, I'm retired,' replied Grandpa Max. 'And so are the Plumbers.'

'Yeah, thanks to you,' Phil said. 'Once you took Vilgax out of the picture, the work just seemed to dry up.'

'Just doing my job.' Grandpa Max shrugged.

'Yeah . . . anyway,' continued Phil, 'looks like things are picking back up again. In fact, I'm starting my own freelance Plumber business . . .' He trailed off when he saw Ben's wrist. 'Wow!' He whistled, his eyes narrowing. 'Cool watch. It looks so familiar . . .'

'It should,' explained Ben. 'It's the Omni–'

'Look at the time!' Grandpa Max said loudly. He caught Ben by the shoulder and began to shove him in the direction of The Rust

Bucket. 'We need to go. Nice catching up with you, Phil. Happy Plumbing!'

�֎ ✖ ✖

The Rust Bucket rattled along a darkened road, Grandpa Max behind the wheel. Ben sat up front, feet on the dashboard, hands behind his head. He looked at his Grandpa Max, confused.

'I don't get it,' he said. 'How come you didn't tell Phil about the Omnitrix?'

'That's on a need-to-know basis only, Ben. The fewer people who know, the better.'

'Guess that's your answer to everything, isn't it, Grandpa Max?' muttered Gwen from somewhere in the back.

'Hey, why don't we start up the Plumbers again?' asked Ben excitedly. 'You, me and Phil. We'd be super alien-butt kickers!'

Grandpa Max sighed and shook his head. 'Ben, I'm flattered you appreciate what I did, but you can't bring back the past.'

Ben opened his mouth to argue, but

a sound from The Rust Bucket's dashboard stopped him. With a faint **BLEEP**, a screen slid out from beneath the instrument panel. It hissed noisily, before blinking into life.

Phil stared out of it. He spoke, his voice urgent and desperate.

'Max, if you're out there, I need help,' he

begged. 'Two Vulpimancers are tearing up a meat-processing plant on Highway Forty-four!'

Grandpa Max's breath caught in his throat. 'Vulpimancers?' he muttered. This wasn't good.

Grandpa Max heaved the campervan round and sped off towards Highway Forty-four.

'All right!' cried Ben as he was bounced around in his seat. 'The Tennysons are back in the Plumbing business!'

🞶 🞶 🞶

From the outside, the meat-processing plant looked just like any other warehouse – even if it didn't sound like one. Savage alien roars tore out through the shattered doors and into the night, as Grandpa Max, Ben and Gwen stepped down from The Rust Bucket.

'I don't like the sound of that,' said Gwen, shivering. Grandpa Max moved past her and silently led the way into the darkened building.

The air inside the plant was icy cold. Their breath formed clouds as Grandpa Max and the two cousins crept along the main corridor where rows of meat hung down from giant hooks.

At the end of the corridor, they found Phil. He was kneeling down by one of the hanging lumps of meat, clutching his ribs.

'Max!' he cried when he saw the approaching Tennysons. 'Thank goodness you showed up. Two aliens. Nasty.' He grinned. 'We're going to need a little of that old magic!'

'No worries,' said Ben, nodding. He ran his fingers over the Omnitrix. 'We're on it.'

**CRASH!** A nearby metal door slammed to the floor, releasing freezing clouds of air into the corridor. As the clouds cleared, two huge shapes clambered through on all fours.

These aliens looked a lot like one of Ben's – the savage Wildmutt – but they were bigger, stronger and more ferocious. They caught the scent of the humans and roared.

Gwen gulped nervously and gave her cousin a nudge. 'Friends of yours?'

# CHAPTER FOUR

# DOGFIGHT

*B*en spun the dial on the Omnitrix.

'Vulpimancers,' he muttered. 'Maybe I can talk to them.'

'Ben!' Grandpa Max began, but the green energy was already swirling round his

grandson, changing him.

'That's why I recognise that watch,' said
Phil in amazement. 'It's the Omnitrix!'

As soon as he had fully transformed,
Wildmutt leaped in front of the oncoming
Vulpimancers. They stopped and bared their
huge fangs at the tiny runt before them.

Unable to actually speak Vulpimancer,
Ben gave a low whine and hoped that it meant
something friendly. The beasts seemed to listen
for a few moments, before the largest threw
back its head and bellowed angrily.

'Vulpimancers never were big on small,'
Grandpa Max said with a gulp.

He watched helplessly as the two
Vulpimancers lunged at Wildmutt. The smaller
alien turned and fled through the processing
plant, but his two bigger cousins set off after
him, snapping at his heels.

Faster and faster Wildmutt ran. He could
smell the two mega-mutts getting closer and
closer. He could feel their heavy footsteps

shaking the room. Any minute now one of them was sure to pounce.

Right on cue, the largest Vulpimancer threw itself forwards. Wildmutt was ready. Leaping upwards, he caught the chain of a dangling meat hook and swung out of the beast's reach. Its sharp claws clacked wildly as it skidded across the floor, unable to stop.

Flailing frantically, the Vulpimancer crashed into a stack of barrels. All four of them toppled, spilling a mound of smelly animal guts down over the savage alien's hairy head.

But Wildmutt wasn't out of danger yet! The second Vulpimancer caught the bottom of the chain he was dangling from and gave it a firm yank. With a creaking of metal, the chain links snapped, and Wildmutt found himself tumbling towards the ground.

Twisting his body, Wildmutt landed on a moving conveyor belt. The mega-mutt slammed hard into him, knocking him on to his back. Then the bigger beast leaped on him, pinning

him in place. Wildmutt howled. The moving
platform was leading them towards a mincing
machine! If he couldn't escape, he was going to
end up as alien burger-meat!

Close by, Phil pressed random buttons
on the plant's control panel. Lights flashed and
machinery whirred into life.

A split second before Wildmutt was
dragged into the spinning blades of the mincer,
the conveyor belt shuddered to a stop. With a
push of a lever, Phil sent a heavy hunk of meat
slamming into the Vulpimancer's side. The alien

yelped as it was sent spinning through the air.

Wildmutt leaped down from the platform, landing next to Phil.

'What are partners for?' The man grinned. Wildmutt nodded his thanks, and the two of them – along with Gwen and Grandpa Max – made a dash for the exit.

Before they could reach safety, the first Vulpimancer stepped into their path. They all turned, ready to retreat, only to find the second alien stalking up behind them. Gwen stared at the beast's enormous fangs and gasped.

'Don't suppose you've ever considered becoming a vegetarian?' she quipped.

Suddenly, a piercing squeal vibrated through the factory. Wildmutt and the Vulpimancers all dropped to the floor, howling in pain as the sound attacked their super-sensitive hearing.

'Sorry about that, Ben,' said Phil, holding up the device emitting the high-pitched sound. 'Only way to bring down a Vulpimancer.'

Grandpa Max eyed the contraption suspiciously. 'Yeah,' he muttered, 'lucky for us you had a sonic pitch whistle with you.'

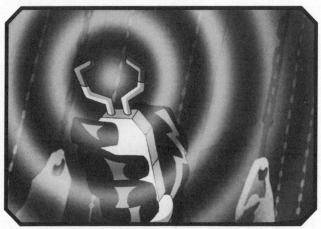

**BLEEP BLEEP BLEEP BLEEEEP!** The Omnitrix suddenly began to flash. Where Wildmutt had stood there was now only Ben, still clutching his aching ears.

'So, all the stories are true,' drawled Phil, 'the Omnitrix really does exist.' He grinned down at Ben. 'Pretty good moves out there. You remind me of your grandfather back in the day.'

'Really?' asked Ben, his eyes wide with wonder.

Behind Phil, one of the Vulpimancers screeched with rage.

'Look out!' cried Grandpa Max, but the warning came too late. The alien swatted the sonic weapon from Phil's hand. As the whistle shattered against the far wall, the factory once again fell silent.

In a split second, the mega-mutts rounded on Phil, hot alien drool dripping from their jagged teeth. This was one meal they were going to enjoy!

'Why don't you pick on someone with more meat on his bones!' boomed Grandpa Max. The aliens turned just in time for a fork-lift truck to thunder into them. Grandpa Max pushed the accelerator pedal to the floor, steering the beasts towards the open door of a wide, walk-in freezer.

Just before the forklift passed through the door, Grandpa Max jumped off. Hitting the ground with a thud, he quickly rolled upright and hit the door's 'close' button. With a mechanical hiss, the metal door swung into place, trapping the aliens inside.

'Just like old times, eh?' Phil smiled. 'I think this is going to be the beginning of a new partnership!'

❈ ❈ ❈

Back at Phil's hotel room, Ben was munching his way through the entire contents of the room-service trolley. This was way better than his grandfather's cooking!

'Ritzy suite!' Grandpa Max whistled, taking in the lavish surroundings. 'Had to cost a pretty penny.'

Phil leaned back in his chair and shrugged. 'Just a little "thank you" I negotiated for helping the manager out with his alien problem. And trust me –' he winked – 'this is just the tip of the iceberg.'

'Y'know, Ben,' he continued, 'you'd make a great Plumber.'

'I would?'

'Sure! A real chip off the old block. We'd make a great team. With your powers, Max's experience and my instincts, we'd be unstoppable!' He turned to Grandpa Max. 'What do you think?'

'I'm thinking,' began Grandpa Max, scratching his chin, 'what an odd coincidence for a Havocbeast and two Vulpimancers to turn up on the same day.'

'Aliens,' said Phil. 'Go figure.'

Grandpa Max stared long and hard at Phil, then turned and headed for the door. 'I need

some fresh air.'

Phil watched the door slam through narrowed eyes. His old partner was up to something. But what?

'Hey, kids,' he said, opening the door again, 'order whatever you'd like off the room-service menu.'

'Now we're talking!' Ben replied, but Phil had already slipped outside.

'Something's going on that Grandpa Max's not telling us about.' Gwen frowned. She stood up and went to follow Phil. 'Come on.'

'And pass up free room service?' Ben spluttered. 'No way, I'm staying here!'

'You're right,' said Gwen slyly. 'It's probably just some secret Plumber mission. Better if we just stay out of it.'

Ben paused, mid-bite. Secret Plumber mission, eh? He liked the sound of that.

❈ ❈ ❈

The wind whipped through the empty car park as Ben and Gwen stepped out through the hotel doors.

'No Grandpa Max,' said Gwen

'And no Phil,' added Ben. 'But where would they go?'

Gwen glanced around. From here she could see all the way down into the nearest town, and all the way up to Mount Rushmore. During their last encounter with Vilgax, Grandpa Max had shown her an underground vault hidden inside the mountain.

'If Grandpa Max thinks that little alien weasel and those space mutts are connected, there's only one place around here to check out!

❀ ❀ ❀

A concealed door clanked open beneath the giant stone head of George Washington, and Grandpa Max stepped into an old Plumber base. It stood empty and silent, its occupants long since gone.

Almost immediately, Grandpa Max's worst fears were confirmed. The Null Void Projector – the Plumbers' single most powerful weapon – had been removed from its case.

'Looking for this?'

Grandpa Max turned to find Phil standing in the doorway, the weapon held tightly in his hand.

'The Null Void Projector.' Grandpa Max scowled. 'I knew those aliens were familiar. You stole the projector to release the ones we caught back in the old days!'

'You always were too smart for your own good, Max.' Phil smirked. 'But not wanting to join up with me was just plain dumb.'

'Why are you doing all this?' Grandpa Max demanded.

'Job security. I release an alien, then get some hotel manager or mayor or whoever to pay me to catch it. Easy money.'

'I'm not going to let you get away with this!'

'Yeah, I figured you might say that.' Phil flipped a switch and the Null Void Projector hummed into life. 'Too bad. We could've made quite a team again.'

A thin beam of yellow energy shot out of the weapon, and Grandpa Max threw himself to the ground. He looked up to see a large portal tearing open just a few metres away.

The hole in space rippled and grew as a huge, monstrous creature pushed its way through. The green-skinned beast snarled, revealing hundreds of gleaming, saw-like teeth.

It scuttled forward on four long legs, each one of which ended with a razor-sharp clawed foot.

Grandpa Max stared, frozen to the spot in horror, as the orc-like creature turned on him and moved in for the kill!

# CHAPTER FIVE

# TRAITOR!

**T**he hulking alien raised one of its deadly claws and aimed a blow at Grandpa Max. A split second before it hit, a black-and-blue blur whipped through the bunker. The orc's foot cracked the rock where Grandpa Max had

been. It screeched as it realised its leg was stuck fast.

Phil spluttered. 'What the –?'

Across the room, XLR8 skidded to a halt, Grandpa Max held safely in his arms.

'You're no Plumber,' he told Phil. 'You're nothing but a big drip!'

'Ben, listen to me,' the traitor begged. 'We don't need your Grandpa Max. We could start the Plumbers back up again, just you and me!'

'Forget it,' XLR8 scoffed, setting his grandfather down. 'And there's nothing you can do to change my mind.'

'Sorry to hear that,' sighed Phil, backing towards the door. His eyes lit up as the hulking green alien finally tore its foot free of the rock. 'Say hello to an old friend,' he cried. 'A Wigzellian Orc Beast!'

The creature swung wildly, its massive claws swiping the air by Grandpa Max's head. XLR8 caught Grandpa Max by the arm and dragged him out of harm's way. He sped towards the metal security door, but Phil slammed it closed behind him, trapping the heroes inside.

XLR8 shot off to battle the Orc Beast. He dodged and weaved past its flailing claws, before landing a hundred punches in less than a second. The Orc Beast barely flinched, launching a counter-attack, which XLR8 only just dodged.

At the far end of the chamber, Grandpa Max slid open a hidden drawer. Reaching inside, he pulled out a weird mechanical object shaped like a mini-umbrella.

'No,' he muttered, replacing the item and opening other drawers. None of them held what he was looking for.

'Grandpa Max, could you pick up the pace?' scowled XLR8, dodging another frenzied attack. Behind him, the Orc Beast tore up a large section of floor and took aim. XLR8 rose up on the balls of his feet, ready to speed out of danger, but –

**BLEEP BLEEP BLEEP BLEEEEP!**

With a red flash from the Omnitrix, XLR8 reverted back to Ben. The chunk of flooring hit him on the chest, knocking him over and pinning him below its weight.

'Got it!' Grandpa Max cried. He pulled a polished silver hand grenade from a drawer and lobbed it towards the Orc Beast. As it connected with the bulky alien, a cloud of green gas hissed from within its metal casing.

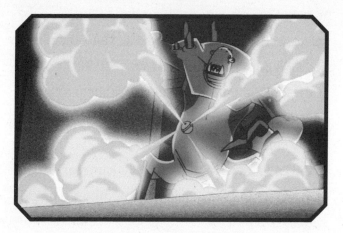

Groaning, the creature slumped to the ground, unconscious. Grandpa Max ran across to his grandson and helped him out from beneath the rubble. The pair dusted themselves

down and looked around the chamber. A
horrible realisation suddenly struck them both.

'Where's Gwen?'

At that moment, Gwen was crouching down low
in the back of Phil's car, wondering what she'd
got herself into. She'd overheard him in the
Plumber base, and decided it would be a good
idea to follow him. Now she wasn't so sure.

'Who says crime doesn't pay?' Phil
chuckled. He sat the Null Void Projector down
on the front passenger seat and turned the key
in the car's ignition. The battered old vehicle
roared as Phil sped off down the mountain track.

Grandpa Max and Ben emerged from the
chamber just as Phil's dust cloud disappeared
down the mountainside. They leaped into The
Rust Bucket and set off in pursuit. Phil's car was
smaller and faster than the campervan though.
They had no chance of catching up. Or did they?

At the flick of a switch, jet turbo engines unfolded from the campervan. Ben was thrown back into his seat as The Rust Bucket shot off at what felt like the speed of sound.

Somewhere up ahead, Gwen made a grab for the Null Void Projector.

'Oh no you don't!' Phil snarled, but Gwen was too fast. She yanked the weapon into the back and began to wind down the window.

'Better start thinking of a new line of work,' she warned, 'because this thing is going bye-bye!'

Phil slammed his hand against the centre of his steering wheel. At once a robotic voice chimed: 'Autopilot engaged.'

The villain clambered into the back as the car continued along the twisty road. Gwen kicked out at him, desperately trying to keep him from the Null Void Projector. As she struggled, the device began to hum. A shimmering portal appeared in the air behind the car.

'Good idea,' smirked Phil as he caught sight of The Rust Bucket tearing along the road behind them. 'We could use a distraction.'

A howling winged creature exploded through the portal and made straight for the first thing it saw – The Rust Bucket. Huge, slimy tentacles wrapped round the front of the vehicle, making it almost impossible for Grandpa Max to see.

'We need some muscle to stop this thing,' Ben cried, adjusting the Omnitrix. 'Four arms of muscle!'

A blinding flash of green light illuminated the inside of the campervan. Grandpa Max glanced at Ben's seat. A tiny bug-eyed alien sat there, blinking in confusion.

'Greymatter?' the little extra-terrestrial cried. 'I said muscle, not miniscule!'

Although small in size, Greymatter was big in the brains department, and he soon had an idea. Scampering up one of the sticky tentacles, he leaped on to the winged creature's back and pulled at flaps of its saggy skin.

'Triggering the correct series of synapses should allow me some rudimentary motor control . . .' he muttered to himself. The part of him that was still Ben shook his head. 'Sure wish I knew what I was talking about.'

With a stamp of his tiny foot, Greymatter struck just the right nerve on the flying beast's back. It dropped The Rust Bucket and began to swoop after the speeding car ahead.

**CRASH!** The full weight of the winged alien smacked down on top of Phil's vehicle, sending it into a wild skid. With a **BANG**, it collided with the metal guard rail at the edge of the road, and came to a shuddering stop.

The abrupt halt sent Greymatter tumbling from the winged beast's back. He bounced hard on the road next to the car, just as Phil came spilling out. Greymatter raised his head to find himself staring down the barrel of the Null Void Projector.

'Back off, small fry,' Phil growled. 'Or I'll release every alien in this thing!'

'Then you'll be out of a job.'

'It doesn't have to be this way,' Phil pleaded. 'We could all work together.'

'No way,' Greymatter spat. 'This is one hero who's not for sale!'

'Well then, you're all going to be very busy!'

Inside the car, Gwen tore down the rear view mirror and threw it to her cousin, just as Phil fired the projector. Greymatter caught it and held it up. It reflected the bright yellow beam, engulfing Phil in a shimmering light.

Phil opened his mouth to scream, but before the sound could emerge, he was gone – sucked forever into the Null Void.

'See ya!' cried Gwen.

Greymatter smiled. 'And I definitely wouldn't want to be ya!'

❋ ❋ ❋

Back inside the secret Plumber base, Grandpa Max shut the Null Void Projector inside its case. The aliens Phil had released had all been taken care of and everything – for the moment – was back to normal.

'I'm sorry I had to keep my past secret for so long,' Grandpa Max said. 'I should've known that I could trust you guys.'

'It's OK.' Gwen shrugged.

'And for what it's worth, Ben, you would've made a great Plumber.' He wrapped his arms round his grandchildren. 'Both of you.'

'Hey, we're your grandkids. What do you expect?' beamed Gwen. She glanced at the Null Void Projector. 'What about Phil?'

Grandpa Max turned and headed for the door, ushering Gwen and Ben out before him. 'I think there are some things in this job we're better off not knowing,' he said.

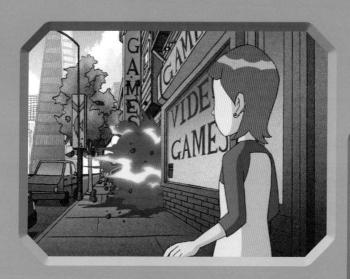

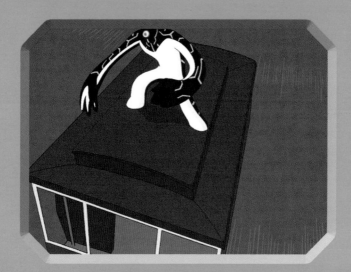

# CHAPTER ONE

# THE FURY OF FOUR ARMS!

*O*n a busy street in downtown San Francisco, Gwen and Grandpa Max stood in a queue, fidgeting impatiently. In front of them, Ben waited quietly, his eyes fixed on the video-game store up ahead. Behind them, the queue seemed to stretch on forever.

'We've been in this line for two hours,' complained Gwen, 'and it hasn't budged an inch!'

Ben didn't take his eyes off the front door of the game shop. 'Small price to pay for Sumo Slammers 2.1!' he told her. 'I'd do anything to get this game – even be seen in public with you!'

'Don't you already have this stupid video game?'

'Hello!' Ben scoffed, turning to face her. 'This is Sumo Slammers 2.1. You can change your fighter's colour at any time during the match. Duh!'

'You know, there is a nice air-conditioned bookstore over there,' said Grandpa Max, diplomatically. 'Maybe we could wait inside until the line thins out a bit.'

'And lose my place?' gasped Ben. 'Not an option. You two go. I'll get my game and meet you guys back at the campervan.'

They didn't need telling twice. Before Ben could change his mind, Grandpa Max and Gwen broke from the line and started towards the bookstore.

'Want us to pick anything up for you?' asked Grandpa Max.

Ben frowned. 'I'm on summer holiday. Why would I read anything?'

Hours later, having spent the afternoon browsing the aisles of the bookshop, Gwen and Grandpa Max stepped out into the San Francisco sunshine.

'So,' said Gwen with a grin, 'think Ben's gone stir crazy in that line yet?'

## KA-RAAASH!

Grandpa Max and Gwen shielded their eyes as the front windows of the video-game

shop exploded outwards, showering the area with deadly shards of glass. A second later, a large, familiar figure leaped out into the street. He clutched a bundle of Sumo Slammers 2.1 video games in his arms. His four arms.

With sirens wailing, a police car skidded round the corner and sped towards the giant red brute. As it neared him, Four Arms reached down and scooped the vehicle up. He shook the car violently until the two policemen inside came tumbling out. They both ran away screaming. They weren't being paid enough to deal with aliens!

'Uh, why is Ben going berserk and tossing around police officers?' asked Gwen, barely able to believe her eyes.

Grandpa Max could only shake his head and shrug. 'Good question.'

A sound like the whirring of a giant fan split the air overhead. Grandpa Max and Gwen looked up to see a helicopter swooping down.

A TV news cameraman leaned out through the side door, capturing all the action on film.

The helicopter banked sharply as a flying lamp post shot up towards it like a javelin. The metal pole narrowly missed, then curved back down towards the ground. Grandpa Max yanked his granddaughter out of the way, just as the lamp post clattered down where she had just stood.

Four Arms spun, fists raised, as a whole platoon of police cars screamed towards him.

Snarling, he caught the front of a nearby parked car and threw it up into the air. It flipped end over end, before smashing into the approaching police vehicles.

'He must've snapped his gap,' Gwen gasped. 'All this for a video game!'

'I don't believe it,' muttered her grandfather. Ben would never behave like this. Would he?

A sleek, black armoured car pulled up beside the Tennysons, its powerful engine humming quietly. They watched, intrigued, as four mean-looking men stepped out. They brushed past Grandpa Max and Gwen, looking for the nearest police officer. They found him cowering behind a mail box.

'Lieutenant Steel, Special Alien Containment Team,' said the largest of the men, flashing the officer his ID badge. 'We'll take it from here.'

Not bothering to wait for a reply, Steel turned to his men and barked: 'Concussion Bazooka!'

The closest soldier leaned inside the armoured vehicle. When he emerged, an enormous cannon was mounted on his shoulder.

'This doesn't look good.' Grandpa Max gulped as he watched the man take aim. Before he could stop her, Gwen ducked past the containment team and sprinted across to Four Arms, who was still tearing the street to pieces.

'Ben, what are you doing?' she demanded.

A large shadow passed over Gwen as Four Arms threw back his powerful fists and brought them down towards her head. She opened her mouth to scream, but the sound was drowned out by the electronic whine of the Concussion Bazooka.

The blast slammed into Four Arms like an express train. It lifted him off his feet and sent him crashing through the front wall of a restaurant on the other side of the street.

'Ben!' Grandpa Max cried, running up and throwing a protective arm round Gwen.

Dust and smoke poured from inside the ruined remains of the restaurant, but nothing else moved. Gwen and Grandpa Max watched, barely daring to breathe, both silently praying for some sign that Ben was alive.

Then, something shifted in the shadows of the shattered shop front. A shape – much larger than any human – stepped through the choking smoke. Everyone watching saw it twist at the waist. They heard it give a grunt of effort. They saw a pizza oven arc across the sky, flames flickering deep within it.

With a deafening **BOOM** the oven hit a parked van and exploded like a bomb. A wall of flames erupted from within it, setting light to everything close by.

As police and civilians alike ran for cover, Four Arms threw up his fists and roared with rage.

Grandpa Max and Gwen could only stand by and watch as the alien tensed his powerful leg muscles, then leaped off over the rooftops.

Grandpa Max glanced around at the utter destruction Four Arms had left in his wake. Ben couldn't have done this. There had to be another explanation for what had just happened.

There had to be!

✷ ✷ ✷

Gwen yanked open the door of The Rust Bucket and flew up the steps in a single bound. Her face was red with rage.

'Are you demented?' she shrieked when she saw Ben sitting at the table. 'Going alien just to get a stupid video game!'

Ben glanced up briefly from his hand-held games console. 'What are you talking about?' he asked, frowning.

'You going four-arm-freaky in front of that

store, that's what I'm talking about!'

'Now, I'm sure he has a good explanation,' said Grandpa Max as he came up the stairs. He

looked over at his grandson hopefully. 'Don't you, Ben?'

'Yeah.' Ben nodded, turning his attention back to Sumo Slammers 2.1. 'I don't know what you're talking about. I haven't done anything wrong.'

'Oh, yeah?' Gwen flicked on the campervan's small TV screen. Ben looked up and found himself watching Four Arms smashing up police cars.

'That's not me!' Ben protested.

'Oh, no, I'm sure it's just some other four-armed alien going crazy in front of a video-game store!'

'It's possible,' said Ben. 'All the alien species in the watch live out in the universe somewhere.'

'That's true,' Grandpa Max agreed. 'Besides, Ben wouldn't be so irresponsible with his alien powers like that.'

'Grandpa Max, please,' scoffed Gwen.

The old man thought about his last comment for a moment. 'All right,' he told Gwen, 'maybe you have a point.'

Ben set his console down on the table and got to his feet. The game would have to wait. Some things were even more important than Sumo Slammers.

Squeezing past Grandpa Max, Ben threw open the door and stomped out of The Rust Bucket.

'No one ruins my alien's reputation,' he seethed. 'Except me!'

........ , ......... ... .... .. ... .... ... ....
... ......... .. .... ..... ...... ..... ... ....
.....

# CHAPTER TWO

## FAMILIAR FACES

**B**en picked his way through the debris outside the video-game store. The street looked like World War III had hit it. Wrecked remains of cars lay burning on the road. Huge chunks of brickwork had crumbled from shop

fronts, smashing holes in the pavement where they'd landed. It was going to take a long time to clean this mess up.

'A criminal always returns to the scene of the crime,' said Gwen, walking behind her cousin.

'Will you give it a rest?' Ben replied. 'I'm trying to solve a mystery here.'

'What do you expect to find that everyone else couldn't?' asked Grandpa Max.

A movement in the shadows of an alleyway caught Ben's eye. There, lurking at the far end of the narrow passage, was a monstrous shape with four powerful arms.

'There he is!' The figure ducked round a corner and Ben set off after him. As he sprinted along the alley, Ben spun the dial on the Omnitrix, searching for the high-speed hero, XLR8. Running made it difficult to see which alien form he was selecting though, so rather than risk changing into Greymatter, he decided just to stay himself.

An out-of-breath Ben staggered out of the other end of the alleyway, his chest aching from the effort of the chase. A big red shape paused on the roof of a nearby building before disappearing inside.

Ben's eyes narrowed as he read the sign above the door of the grand, imposing building.

'The Mint!' he gasped. The fake Four Arms had just broken into a building where huge amounts of money were printed. That could only be bad news!

As Ben charged off in the direction of the US Mint building, Grandpa Max and Gwen skidded out of the alley behind him. Grandpa Max stumbled along unsteadily, barely able to keep up with his speeding grandchildren.

He stopped for a moment to catch his breath and wipe the sweat from his brow. 'Who said,' he gasped, 'that retirement was relaxing?'

❈ ❈ ❈

A few moments later, Grandpa Max, now able to breathe, sneaked into the main printing room of the Mint with Gwen.

Long sheets of paper whizzed through printers – going in blank and emerging as hundreds of millions of dollars. Coins slid from stamping machines into transport trolleys, their metal still hot to the touch. But Ben was nowhere to be seen.

'Are you sure he came in here?' asked Grandpa Max.

As if in answer to his question, a huge fireball lit up the room. Grandpa Max and Gwen darted round a corner to find Heatblast scaring off two security guards with a jet of flickering flame.

'OK, I was willing to give him one,' Gwen seethed, 'but two of Ben's aliens terrorising San Francisco? That can't be a coincidence, Grandpa Max. I'm stopping this right now!'

Not waiting for a reply, she turned and stomped off towards the fiery alien.

'Yo, hothead,' she cried, 'back off the fireworks before someone gets hurt.' She glared up at Heatblast and folded her arms in front of her. 'Now, if you take responsibility for all the whacko stuff you've been doing lately, I'm sure we can help you.'

'Uh, Gwen,' came a voice from behind her.

'Not now, dweeb,' she sighed. 'Can't you see I've got a . . .' Her voice trailed off as she realised who the voice belonged to. 'Ben?' But, if her cousin was behind her, that meant . . .

'So, who are you?' she asked, taking a step away from the fake Heatblast.

'Me?' growled the alien, his hands turning white with heat as he spoke. 'I'm a hottie, can't you tell?'

A plume of flame leaped from his fingertips. Gwen closed her eyes, unable to get out of the way in time. She heard something heavy hitting the ground in front of her. When she opened her eyes again, Diamondhead stood before her, shielding her from the fire.

'Now do you believe me?' Ben snapped as he launched a spray of dart-like diamonds towards Heatblast. He nodded in the direction of the guards. 'You and Grandpa Max get everyone else out of here.'

While Gwen and Grandpa Max led the guards to safety, a few more fireballs bounced off Diamondhead's body. He turned to face his attacker, only to discover the fake Heatblast had vanished.

'I don't know who you are,' Diamondhead growled, his voice echoing around the inside of the Mint, 'but you're giving aliens a bad name.'

'So why don't you cry about it?' sneered Heatblast from somewhere close by. 'Or are you going to run and tell on me to your Grandpa Max, or that smart-mouth cousin of yours?'

Diamondhead stopped, stunned. His mind

raced. How did this impostor know so much about his life? They'd never met before. Had they?

Suddenly, a blast of flames struck one of the trolleys that swung from the roof, carrying thousands of coins across the room. The metal casing exploded, and a stream of money poured down on Diamondhead, knocking him off his feet. As the hero tried to clamber free of the mountain of coins, Heatblast stepped out from behind a printing press.

'Hey, it's raining money!' he cried.

'Who are you?' Diamondhead demanded. Heatblast snorted.

'You still haven't figured it out?' he scoffed. 'Maybe this'll help.'

Before Diamondhead's eyes, the other alien's head began to change shape. First it stretched to look like XLR8. Next it became Ripjaws. It quickly went through every one of Ben's aliens, before stopping on a face that was chillingly familiar.

This face was human. Or, at least, it used to be.

'Kevin?' Diamondhead gasped.

Ben had met Kevin earlier in the summer, and they'd quickly become friends. That is until Kevin stole Ben's powers and tried to kill a trainful of people. That kind of thing can break even the strongest of friendships.

Last time they'd fought, Ben had barely survived. This time, Kevin seemed to be more powerful than ever.

'I don't get it,' Diamondhead said, getting up to face his enemy. 'I thought you were drained of all my power back in the subway in New York.'

'That's what you get for thinking, Benji,' Kevin spat. 'Turns out I absorbed enough of the weird watch energy that I could turn into any of those aliens, if I just concentrated hard enough.' His eyes narrowed into thin slits. 'Only problem is now I can only stay human for a short time. You made me into this freak!'

'Like this is my fault?' Diamondhead growled. 'Whose idea was it to drain out all the powers of the watch? Not mine!'

'I don't care,' Kevin snarled, 'cos now it's payback time, "partner". Everything fifty-fifty. I do the crime and you'll do the time!'

'You'll never get away with this.'

'Wrong!' cried Kevin. 'You'll never get away with this! I'm not me. I'm you. Remember?'

A volley of laser fire brought one of the building's windows crashing in. A squad of Alien Containment Troops came clambering through.

'Keep the change!' Kevin grinned, throwing a handful of coins at Diamondhead. 'You can use it to pay your bail.'

He gritted his teeth and concentrated. Within moments, he'd morphed into the insect-like Stinkfly.

'Gotta fly!' he hissed. Diamondhead could only watch as Stinkfly-Kevin sliced upwards and escaped through a hole in the Mint's glass ceiling.

A platoon of soldiers rushed to surround Diamondhead, their weapons trained on him. Lieutenant Steel stepped between them, stopping directly in front of the captive alien.

'Sorry, rock-head,' he growled. 'No unauthorised withdrawals on my watch!'

## CHAPTER THREE

# RUNAWAY CABLE CAR

**D**iamondhead backed away from Steel, his eyes fixed on the gun the man held.

'You don't get it,' he protested. 'The bad alien just got away. I'm the good alien!'

'Yeah, sure you are. Just like those "alien heroes" all over the news nowadays.' Steel raised his weapon. 'No sale. To me you're just a walking chandelier.'

'He's telling the truth, officer,' said Gwen as she and Grandpa Max burst through the doors. 'There was another alien who –'

'I don't try 'em, kid; I just catch 'em.' Steel shrugged. 'We'll let the boys at Area Fifty-one figure out who's naughty and who's nice.'

Behind Steel, a dozen soldiers trained their weapons on Diamondhead.

'Chicago, Tallahassee, Barstow,' said the commander, counting off the cities on his fingers. 'You and your outer-space pals have been keeping me real busy, but you're not getting away with it this time.'

Diamondhead frowned. This time? What did he mean?

There was no time to think about it now. If he were going to escape, he had to act fast. With a flick of his wrist, he launched a handful of diamond missiles towards the Alien Containment Team. The deadly shards sliced through their laser guns, causing them to explode, spraying sparks and smoke in all directions.

Seizing his chance, Diamondhead ran through the thick, black plumes, dodging sprays of gunfire from those soldiers who still had weapons.

'Get that thing!' Steel roared, stabbing a finger in the fleeing alien's direction.

Diamondhead skidded round a corner and stopped by some heavy machinery. If he could find somewhere to hide, maybe he would change back to Ben before he was discovered. But when you're a giant alien made of green diamond finding a hiding place isn't easy.

A red dot appeared on his broad chest. He peered down at it, watching it shimmer back and forth just above his stomach. It was a few seconds before the terrible realisation hit him. The red dot was coming from a laser targeting system! Someone had him in their sights!

**KRRR-ZZZAP!** A crackling energy blast struck him hard. Its force slammed him down on to the ground. As the concrete floor shattered, it threw up a billowing cloud of dust, engulfing the fallen alien.

High up on a metal walkway, two soldiers exchanged a high five. They'd done it. They'd brought him down. They'd probably get a promotion for this.

A razor-sharp shard of diamond sliced through the air between them and embedded itself into the wall with a faint crack. The soldiers gulped nervously and peered over the edge of the railing. Diamondhead stood below, staring back up. He winked, before spraying several more shards of diamonds up towards the walkway.

The slivers of precious stone sliced through the metal railing, and both men soon found themselves tumbling to the ground below. They thudded down, one on top of the other. For a moment they thought about moving, but decided that staying where they were might be the safest option.

Footsteps clacked along the concrete somewhere behind Diamondhead. The alien turned, ready to fight, but a horribly familiar bleeping forced him to rethink his plans. The Omnitrix was flashing red. Any minute now he was going to change back!

Steel rounded the corner, gun raised and ready. His finger tightened on the trigger for a moment, before relaxing. Lowering his weapon, he glared down at the small boy cowering on the floor, his eyes tightly shut.

'Don't hurt me!' Ben begged. Slowly, he opened one eye. 'Oh,' he said, trying his best not to grin. 'Is that monster gone?'

‘Oh, thank goodness you found him!’ cried Gwen, as Steel and the soldiers led Ben out into the fresh air. ‘We were so worried. He’s always wandering away. We’re considering getting a leash.’

Steel sighed and shoved Ben in the direction of his waiting family. As he did, his eyes fell on the Omnitrix.

‘Nice watch,’ he said. ‘Never seen anything like it.’

‘Yeah,’ Ben said, hiding it behind his back. ‘It’s from, ah . . . Japan.’

‘No sign of the alien, sir,’ announced a soldier as he emerged from the Mint. ‘It’s like that thing disappeared into thin air.’

Steel clenched his jaw, making the thick muscles on his neck stand out. He glared at the Tennysons. ‘I don’t suppose you three know anything about this alien?’

'No,' said Grandpa Max quickly. 'If we did, we'd tell you.'

Steel's eyes narrowed. 'Yeah. Of course you would.'

The man performed a sharp about-turn and began marching away, much to Ben's relief. Talk about a narrow escape!

'Keep an eye on them,' Steel told a soldier, when they were out of the Tennysons' earshot. 'They know more than they're saying.'

※ ※ ※

Back in The Rust Bucket, Ben filled Grandpa Max and Gwen in on everything he'd learned. Gwen's fingers flitted over the keys of her laptop as she listened. Ben could never understand how she managed to hold a conversation and type at the same time. If he was honest, it kind of creeped him out.

'It was Kevin at both the video-game store and the Mint,' Ben told them. 'They were set-ups!'

'That would explain a lot,' said Grandpa Max with a nod. 'I don't mind telling you, that kid's rowboat is missing a couple of paddles.'

'But why does the swat-team guy think all aliens are bad?' asked Ben.

'Looks like from personal experience,' said Gwen. 'Check this out.'

She spun the laptop round, revealing a scanned newspaper article. The photograph showed Ripjaws attacking a group of panicked civilians. 'Your friend has been busy,' Gwen continued. 'And not just here in San Francisco. Wildmutt terrorising Tallahassee. Ripjaws in Chicago. Ghostfreak in Barstow . . .'

'I'm going to get blamed for all that stuff,' Ben cried. 'And I didn't do any of it!'

Suddenly, a loud grinding noise coming from outside caught their attention. All three occupants of The Rust Bucket huddled together to peer through a side window. What they saw chilled them to the bone.

One of San Francisco's famous trams – a vehicle pulled along the streets by a thick underground steel rope – was speeding down a steep hill. Inside, the passengers screamed, trapped and helpless. Outside, the normally red cable car shone with a black-and-green alien sheen.

'Kevin!' Ben spat.

'The boy must've gone Upgrade to hijack that tram,' Grandpa Max gasped.

Ben leaped up from his seat and adjusted the Omnitrix. 'Anything he can upgrade, I can upgrade better!'

With a blinding flash of green, Ben transformed. He felt the rough fur covering his body and groaned.

'Wildmutt?' snorted Gwen. 'Nice choice, Fido.'

The alien canine gave a yelp of frustration before throwing open the door of the campervan and bounding along the street after the tram.

※ ※ ※

Up on a nearby rooftop, an Alien Containment soldier pressed the button on the side of his walkie-talkie. 'Mobile One. A wild-dog alien just emerged from the campervan. Now both are heading down California Street.'

Steel's voice hissed over the radio. 'Maintain visual. I'm on my way.'

✖ ✖ ✖

Inside the speeding tram, the driver struggled with the brake lever. Behind him, terrified tourists screamed and clawed at the windows, desperately trying to escape.

'Now why are you doing that?' said a voice from the front of the car. Two snaking coils unfolded from the dashboard. They wrapped round the brake lever, wrenched it from the driver's grasp, and snapped it in half.

'We're just starting to have fun!'

**THUD!** Wildmutt landed on the roof of the tram. Almost at once, the metal below his feet rearranged itself to form Upgrade's face. 'Sorry, Ben,' Kevin cackled. 'No pets allowed!'

A large metal spike exploded upwards from the roof, stabbing into Wildmutt's paws. The dog-like alien howled with pain and leaped sideways. His sharp claws dug deep into the side of the tram, enabling him to swing in through the driver's window. **CRASH!**

The screaming tourists screamed even louder when they saw the savage beast come clattering through the window. The noise dazed Wildmutt, overwhelming his alien senses, and he didn't notice the two heavy benches until they were slammed down hard on his head.

'Heel, boy, heel!' laughed Upgrade-Kevin, as he stared down at his trapped foe. 'There's a good hero!'

Concentrating hard, Kevin released his control over the tram and returned to normal.

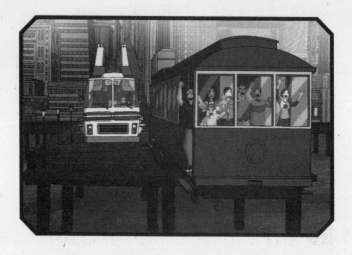

Back in human form on the roof of the tram, he could see the rapidly approaching San Francisco Bay. Any minute now, the people in the tram would be going for their last swim.

'Let's see,' he muttered. 'Brakes are out, hero's trapped and everyone's about to go for a dip in the bay.' Groaning with the pain of the effort, Kevin morphed into Stinkfly and buzzed into the sky. 'I'd say my work here is done!'

## CHAPTER FOUR

# CLASH OF THE TITANS

**WOOOOOSH!** The Rust Bucket roared along the street, its hidden jet engines fully unfolded and engaged. Grandpa Max grinned, enjoying the thrill of the chase.

'Times like these my demolition derby experience really comes in handy!'

He eased down on the brake as they caught up with the runaway tram. Leaning out of his window, Grandpa Max pointed at a cable and hook, which were attached to the back of the tram.

'Ben, attach the line to the bottom of the campervan!' he cried.

Wildmutt clambered out of the back of the tram and took the metal hook in his powerful jaws. With a short bound, he landed on The Rust Bucket. It took him just a moment to set the hook in place.

Gwen gripped her seat as Grandpa Max slammed down hard on the brakes. Smoke poured from the tyres as the line tying the two vehicles together became tight. It wasn't enough though. The tram was still hurtling towards the water, and now it was dragging The Rust Bucket along with it! There were only seconds left until they all took the plunge.

One chance. They still had one chance! Grandpa Max flicked a switch on the dashboard then clamped his hands down on the steering wheel. Things were about to get scary.

With a hiss, a gas-propelled anchor launched from the back of The Rust Bucket. It rocketed backwards along the street before punching a hole straight through the side of a building. Wide metal prongs sprang out, locking the device in place.

Gwen screamed as the anchor line pulled tight. The sudden stop threw her forward, and only her safety belt stopped her crashing through the front windscreen.

When she'd recovered, Gwen raised her head enough to look out through the window. Up ahead, at the other end of the metal rope, stood the cable car. Its front end dangled dangerously out over the water, but everyone inside was safe.

They'd done it! They'd foiled Kevin's plan just in the nick of time.

❉ ❉ ❉

A few minutes later, when both vehicles had been untangled, Grandpa Max and Gwen found Ben hiding round a corner. He'd only just transformed back from Wildmutt, and was still wiping the dust from his hands.

Gwen smiled at him. 'Not bad for an alien with no thumbs,' she admitted.

'Freeze!' barked a voice from behind them. The Tennysons turned to find themselves surrounded by the Special Alien Containment Team. Lieutenant Steel snarled as he stepped forward. 'One move and you're all Swiss cheese.'

Grandpa Max, Gwen and Ben all took a step back, half-blinded by the spotlight being shone down on them from a helicopter that circled above.

'You have two choices,' Steel warned them. 'Tell me what you have to do with these aliens, or get measured for your prison uniforms.' He caught Ben's arm and examined the Omnitrix. 'It has something to do with this watch, doesn't it?' Steel demanded. 'Is it some kind of signal to call the aliens?'

'Sir!' cried the nearest soldier. 'We're getting reports of a crystal alien rampaging on the Golden Gate. Looks like it could bring the whole bridge down if it isn't stopped.'

Steel hesitated. These people knew something, he was sure. Still, the alien had to be stopped before he could cause any more damage. 'Falcon One,' he said into his radio. 'Pick me up.' Overhead, the helicopter swung round on his command. The lieutenant glared down at Ben. 'We're not done.'

Watching the soldiers jump into the helicopter, Ben spun the dial on the Omnitrix. 'Those guys don't stand a chance against Kevin,' he said. 'I have to stop him!'

❈ ❈ ❈

High on the vast metal supports of the Golden Gate Bridge, Kevin was hard at work. He had transformed into Diamondhead, and was using the alien's sharp hands to slice through the cables holding the giant construction together.

Down below, the road began to sway more and more with each cable Kevin sliced.

Soon it would collapse completely, sending hundreds of innocent people tumbling to their doom.

A wind whipped at the villain from nowhere. He looked up and saw the SACT helicopter swooping down towards him. Lieutenant Steel hung below it, winching himself down to face the alien menace.

Kevin responded with a volley of diamond missiles. They clipped the tail of the helicopter, sending it into an uncontrollable spin.

'All right!' he cheered, as he watched the aircraft plunge towards the road below.

Swinging wildly, Steel sliced the rope that held him. He fell, hand reaching for his pistol, and landed on top of the metal support, directly in front of a startled Kevin.

Down below, the helicopter thwacked into the road. Luckily, some of the cables had slowed its fall, and all of the soldiers tumbled out, unhurt.

'Lieutenant Steel,' Kevin growled. 'So nice to see you again.'

❈ ❈ ❈

The Rust Bucket weaved past a group of police cars and sped on to the swaying bridge. All around it, people screamed and fled in the opposite direction, trying to get clear before the structure gave way.

Ben leaped from the campervan. He sighed when he saw the damage that had already been done to the bridge.

'Just one more thing I'm going to get blamed for!'

※ ※ ※

Lieutenant Steel flew backwards and slammed solidly against part of the metal structure. He dropped to his knees, fighting for breath. His face was a mass of cuts and bruises. He was losing the fight. Badly.

Diamondhead-Kevin reached down and jerked the officer off the ground. He held him against the main bridge support and pulled back his other arm, ready to deliver one final, devastating punch.

'Let him go, Kevin!'

Kevin turned, Steel still held in one hand.

Four Arms crouched on top of the next support pillar, poised and ready for action. 'This is about you and me,' the hero growled.

Kevin shrugged. 'Sounds good to me.' He hurled his limp prisoner away. Steel threw out his hands, barely managing to catch hold of a cable. Muscles burning from the effort, he pulled himself up on to a narrow platform and waited for his strength to return.

'Still trying to be a goody two shoes, Ben?' Kevin snickered. 'Let me guess – you just want to help me.'

'You had plenty of chances to get help, but you always messed it up.' Four Arms narrowed both pairs of yellow eyes. 'This time, you're getting what you deserve.'

'Aww, does this mean we're not best buddies any more?' said Kevin sarcastically. He cackled maniacally as he unleashed a spray of diamonds in Four Arms' direction.

The big red alien somersaulted over the attack and landed at his enemy's feet.

**KA-RUNCH!** A powerful uppercut sent
Kevin crashing backwards into a support pillar.

'You risked all those innocent lives just
to get even with me!' snapped Four Arms,
advancing.

'Nobody's innocent!' Kevin screeched,
jumping to his feet. 'They just haven't had a
chance to make fun of me yet!'

Down beside the wreckage of the helicopter, two soldiers took aim with the Concussion Bazooka. Their sights were trained on the aliens, who were now locked in battle.

'You can't do this!' Gwen protested. 'He's trying to help!'

'Targets locked on, sir,' barked the trooper into his radio. 'Permission to fire?'

Steel opened his swollen eyes and watched the aliens clashing violently. Something was different about the red one. Something he wasn't quite sure of. He unclipped his walkie-talkie from his belt.

'Fire on my command only,' he said. 'Repeat. On my command only.'

Four Arms ducked a swinging punch and caught Diamondhead-Kevin by the throat. With a grunt of effort he yanked the villain into the air, before slamming him down hard on to the ground.

Kevin's body instantly began to morph. A jet of flame shot up from his fingers as he

changed into Heatblast. The fire hit Four Arms in the face, temporarily blinding him.

Eyes stinging, Four Arms lashed out. A flailing fist caught Heatblast-Kevin as he stood up, sending him soaring into the sky. Changing so quickly was difficult – and painful – but Kevin managed to transform into Stinkfly and slow himself down.

The insect alien looped twice to build up speed, then rocketed down towards the still half-blinded Four Arms. He was going to knock the hero right off the edge, and end this thing once and for all!

# CHAPTER FIVE

# ALL CHANGE

**A**s Kevin swooped down towards Four Arms, something began to happen to him. A sharp, shooting pain coursed through his body. His pincer-like claws shrank and altered, twisting into five stubby fingers. His wings stopped flapping and curled down into his body.

And then suddenly, in a blur of limbs, he changed completely. Several hundred feet above sea level, he cried out in horror as he realised he was no longer Stinkfly-Kevin. Nor was he Heatblast-Kevin. He wasn't even Diamondhead-Kevin. He was just Kevin, plain and simple. And he was falling fast!

**BA-DOING!** The tumbling Kevin struck Four Arms on the chest and bounced off. The big red alien peered down at the eleven-year-old boy who lay in a crumpled heap at his feet. Roaring, Four Arms threw two of his arms above his head, then swung them back down. His fists connected with a deafening BOOM!

Cowering, Kevin flicked open one eye. On either side of his head, deep fist-shaped dents had been hammered into the metal. He opened the other eye and raised his head. Four Arms was walking away, the battle – as far as he was concerned – well and truly over.

'Get back here and fight, Tennyson,' Kevin cried. 'I'm not through with you yet!'

Four Arms paused. 'But I'm through with you,' he said, his voice as dry and coarse as gravel. 'You're not worth it. You never were.'

Kevin scrambled back up, his face contorting in rage. How dare Tennyson speak to him like that? Everyone always made fun of him. Everyone called him a freak. There was no way he was letting Ben walk away. No way!

The hatred and the fury burned through Kevin's veins. As they did, another transformation began to take place. He gasped as something seemed to explode inside him, pushing his chest forwards and forcing his shoulders out.

Kevin threw back his head and tried to scream, but a terrible, inhuman roar burst from his lips, which had become bloated and cracked.

The skin on his back blistered and split as two Stinkfly wings emerged. Kevin wasn't changing into the insect alien though. He was changing into . . . something else. Something new.

Four Arms watched in horror as Kevin continued to mutate. A Wildmutt arm grew from the villain's ribs. Then a Diamondhead arm sprouted from his shoulder. His legs, too, became as red and muscled as Four Arms's own. A long XLR8 tail snaked down his spine.

Most hideous of all, however, was his face. Nothing about it was Kevin's. Instead, it was a patchwork quilt of mismatched eyes, jagged teeth and spindly antennae.

Kevin clenched his fists and concentrated, desperately trying to change back, desperately trying to be normal.

'I-I can't change back!' he wailed at last. 'I'm . . . I'm stuck like this!' He rounded on Four Arms, his massive frame towering over the heroic alien. 'Look at what you've done!' he bellowed.

Oh, man, thought Ben. Is there anything I'm not going to get blamed for today?

A thunderous punch to the head brought his train of thought crashing to a halt. Kevin drove a knee sharply into Four Arms's stomach, knocking the wind from his body. A lightning-fast tail whipped round, knocking the hero's feet from under him.

Four of the strongest arms on the planet stretched out, as the alien tried desperately to catch on to the bridge. He tumbled backwards over the edge, plummeting towards certain doom.

One hand finally found something to grab. With a jerk, Four Arms came to an sudden stop, dangling more than two hundred metres above the water. A shadow loomed over him as Kevin shambled over to the edge.

'You'll never beat me,' Kevin snarled. 'Because you're one of the good guys. And good guys never have the guts to finish guys like me!'

'But I do!' barked Lieutenant Steel from the nearby ledge. He jabbed his finger against the button on his walkie-talkie and yelled: 'Fire!'

The blast of the Concussion Bazooka scorched up through the air, covering the distance from the bottom of the bridge to the top in a heartbeat. The beam drove Kevin backwards. He thrashed frantically, but was too late to stop himself falling.

Watched by dozens of onlookers, Kevin dropped from the bridge, and plummeted into the icy cold waters below.

Four Arms dragged himself up on to the bridge and leaped across to where Lieutenant Steel was struggling upright. The soldier glared at the hulking alien, but made no move to attack.

'Are you still looking for me?' asked Four Arms.

'Second target locked on,' crackled a voice over the walkie-talkie. 'Permission to fire?'

Steel hesitated, the radio held close to his mouth. The events of the last few minutes were a painful blur, but he reckoned he could pretty much piece together what had been happening.

'We got our alien,' he said. 'Stand down.'

Four Arms nodded. That was exactly what he'd been hoping to hear. With a twitch of his gigantic legs, the alien bounded off across the bridge, making his getaway before the watch decided to time out on him again.

Steel leaned forwards and peered over the edge. The ground seemed a long way away.

'Well, what are you waiting for?' he barked into his radio. 'Pretty please? Get me down!'

❈ ❈ ❈

Twenty minutes later, all three Tennysons strapped themselves into their usual seats in The Rust Bucket. Every part of Ben ached. He was going to be covered in bruises for a week! Still, at least they were all out of danger. For now.

'Not even Kevin could have survived that blast and that fall,' said Gwen. 'Right?'

'You're asking the wrong guy,' Ben sighed. 'I thought he was gone for good last time.'

Grandpa Max slipped the campervan into gear and began to pull out into the slow moving procession of traffic. A bruised and battered figure in military uniform stepped in front, blocking the way. Steel approached the passenger window and knocked hard on the glass.

'Now why is it,' he began, when Ben wound down the window, 'that you three are always around when aliens show up?'

'Really,' said Grandpa Max, 'is that a fact? We hadn't noticed.'

'Yeah, guess it's just coincidence,' replied Steel suspiciously, his eyes narrowed. He stepped back from the campervan, making room for it to pass. 'Maybe we'll cross paths again some time. Drive carefully. Lots of weird stuff out there.'

Ben grinned. 'Yeah,' he said. 'You're telling us!'

Steel watched The Rust Bucket drive away, weaving past police cars and burning wreckage as it headed off the bridge, and towards whatever adventure awaited it.

In the water beneath the bridge, unseen by any of the people above, a cluster of bubbles rose to the surface and burst.

Something was down there – and it was still very much alive . . .